FORTUNE T̶ Club

THE
LOST
GIRL

FORTUNE TELLERS Club

THE LOST GIRL

DOTTI ENDERLE

2002
Llewellyn Publications
St. Paul, Minnesota 55164-0383, U.S.A.

FIRST EDITION
First printing, 2002

Book design and editing by Kimberly Nightingale
Cover design by Kevin R. Brown
Cover illustration and interior illustrations © 2002 by Matthew Archambault

Library of Congress Cataloging-in-Publication Data
(Pending)

ISBN: 0-7387-0253-6

Llewellyn Publications
A Division of Llewellyn Worldwide, Ltd.
P.O. Box 64383, Dept. 0-7387-0253-6
St. Paul, MN 55164-0383, U.S.A.
www.llewellyn.com

Printed in the United States of America

For Doris Wade Varley

Special thanks to Lynne McCloskey and Jo Ellen Kucera

Contents

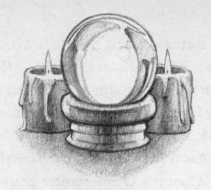

CHAPTER 1

A Matter of Life and Death

Determined, Juniper sat up tall, positioning the planchette on the Ouija board. "Let's try again, Gena. This time, concentrate!"

Gena took a deep breath, nodding. Neither girl spoke the question out loud since this was their third attempt. They placed their fingers lightly on the planchette. Juniper closed her eyes and cleared her mind. A mysterious feeling rippled through her. It was that same tingling she always had whenever she worked the Ouija board, or any of her other fortune telling tools. She couldn't explain it, but it had always been there. Her mom called it the gift, a psychic trait passed down in the family from mother to daughter from generations back.

Please tell us where Gena lost her retainer! Juniper thought. When the Ouija pointer skated to the left, Juniper opened her eyes. It spelled P–A–R–K.

Gena slumped.

"It's the same answer," Juniper said. "That has to be right."

"It can't be," Gena argued. "I haven't been to the park since the last day of school. Besides, why would I take my retainer out there?"

"Maybe you dropped it when you were running from that squirrel."

"What squirrel?" Gena asked.

"The one that thought you were a nut!"

Laughter came floating up from behind a magazine. Their friend, Anne, had been lying on the bed listening.

"Okay," Anne said, tugging on her too short shorts. "Tomorrow we'll ride our bikes to the park and look around."

"It can't be at the park!" Gena complained.

"Well, then pull that Ouija board around here and let me try." Anne said. "Maybe I can word the question a little differently."

"Oh, sure," Gena said. "I know what your question would be." She draped the back of her hand across her forehead for dramatic flair. "Which guy at school really likes me?"

Anne rolled her eyes. "School's out, Gena. I'm only concentrating on the guys at the pool."

"Come on," Juniper said, her voice softening. "This is why we formed the Fortune Tellers Club. To help each other out at a time like this."

★ ★ ★

Juniper, Anne, and Gena had been friends since elementary school. No three girls could be more different, yet the connection was made the day Juniper brought her Magic 8-Ball to school.

"What's that for?" Anne had whispered, leaning across her desk.

"We have a true-false quiz today," Juniper whispered back. "I thought I could double-check my answers before turning it in."

"*Cheat?*" Anne blurted.

"Shhhhh!" Juniper said, putting her finger to her mouth. "I don't think of it as cheating. It's more like foreseeing the answers."

Anne raised an eyebrow. "Do you think it will work?"

"There's one way to find out."

Cradling the shiny black globe in her hands, Juniper rocked it back and forth a few times. The usual tingling that circulated through her when she held the 8-ball just wasn't there. She paused, then turned it over. The triangular message floated slowly to the surface. *Try again later.*

"You didn't shake it hard enough," Anne whispered a little too loudly.

Juniper rolled her eyes. "You don't shake fortune telling objects, silly. You'll shake all the cosmic vibrations out." Was she the only person around who understood these things?

Gena, who was sitting directly in front of Juniper, turned around. "You should ask it what's going to happen to you if you get caught."

Anne snickered, but Juniper ignored the remark.

Gena crossed her arms. "If you're such an expert fortune teller, then why didn't you just bring your crystal ball?"

Juniper's mind drifted to the New Age shop and the Gypsy-style crystal ball displayed in the window. It sat on a pillow of deep blue velvet and reminded her of the moon reflected on water. But the price tag reminded her that she'd never have enough money to own it. She sighed. "Because that's the one form of divination I don't have."

"*Divi*-what?" Anne asked.

"Divination. You know, fortune telling stuff." Juniper slipped the 8-ball into her desk and covered it with her open social studies book.

"You mean you have more of this stuff at home?" Anne seemed curious.

"Sure," Juniper answered. "Cards, wands, dice."

Anne and Gena moved in closer. Juniper had no doubt that she held their interest.

"Why don't you come over after school and take a look?"

They did, and two years later, the Fortune Tellers Club was still going strong.

★ ★ ★

"She's right," Gena said to Anne. "The Fortune Tellers Club was formed for times like this. And if I don't find my retainer, my dad is going to kill me!"

Juniper wanted nothing more than to help Gena out. Psychically locating lost things was part of her *gift*. Why was it so different this time?

"Well, give us a clue here, Gena," Juniper said. "Did you take it out when you went to sleep?"

"Oh, no, I have to sleep in that awful thing."

"I *know* you take it out to eat," Anne said.

"But I always put it back in."

"Maybe *park* means something else," Juniper said, her mind racing for an answer.

"Like what?" Gena asked.

"Like *park*ing lot or *park*ing garage."

"Or *Park* Place Drive," Gena chimed in, her eyes lit with understanding.

"Or *Park*er Station," Anne said, nodding.

"See," Juniper assured her friend. "We have a lot of places to investigate tomorrow. How long can you hold off before you have to tell your dad?"

Gena gave a halfhearted shrug. "I don't know. I think I can get by until this weekend."

"Fine then," Juniper said, "There's nothing to worry about."

Gena shot forward. "Nothing to worry about! We just have a few clues, and even those aren't that great. I haven't been out to Parker Station since we took my aunt out there last week. Come on, Juniper, you're the expert. Where is it?"

Juniper rubbed her face in frustration. "I don't know, but there's got to be a way to pinpoint the exact location."

She pulled a library book out from under a stack of magazines next to her CD player. The title read *The Future Is In Your Hands: Techniques For*

Fortune Telling. "Let's look through here to see if we can find a new method."

The girls clumsily skimmed the pages.

"Look," Gena said, "according to this book you can see the future in a glass of water." She pointed to a page that showed a woman peering into a goblet of water. The woman held her palms against her cheeks, and she looked like she'd just won a million-dollar jackpot.

"They call it *scrying,*" Anne said, running her finger over the text. "It's the same thing as crystal gazing."

"So let's try it!" Juniper yelled, darting toward the bedroom door.

"Wait!" Anne called. "Get a bowl instead of a glass. That way we can all gaze into it."

Juniper raced out to the kitchen. She chose a clear glass bowl, then filled it to the rim. Walking back slowly, heel to toe, she was careful not to spill a single drop. And she was doubly careful as she set it down on the night table in her bedroom.

All three girls stood there, staring at the bowl as though it might jump up and start dancing at any minute. Then Juniper sat on the edge of her bed.

"Okay . . . here goes."

She leaned forward and gazed down into the bowl. Her heartbeat quickened. She might as well have been opening a door to another universe. The water rippled and a drop slid down the side.

"Hold still," Juniper complained.

"Sorry," Gena said, taking a step back. She folded her hands in a prayer position. "Please don't let my retainer be in the bottom of the dumpster at Funtime Pizza," she whispered.

Then—silence. No one moved. No dogs barked outside. No birds sang. And in the silence, Juniper held her breath.

She stared hard, not sure whether the future would appear at the top or the bottom of the bowl. But she knew it had to work. Her vision blurred a few times, but she never took her eyes off the water. That mysterious feeling filled her, and seemed to send electricity through her veins. Then it happened. An image rose to the top of the bowl as slowly and surely as the message at the bottom of her Magic 8-Ball.

"Oh my gosh," Juniper cried. "I see something."

CHAPTER 2

The Girl in
the Glass Bowl

I s it my retainer?" Gena asked.
"No, it's a girl," Juniper said.

"Is she *wearing* my retainer?"

Juniper didn't answer. She continued to gaze into the bowl of water. The pale face of a young girl gazed back. Juniper had never seen the girl, but her face had a familiar, haunting look.

Juniper strained to keep her focus. Her eyes began to sting. She was afraid if she blinked the image would disappear, and she had to know what this meant. Who was this girl? Was she real? Tears began to pool on Juniper's bottom lashes. She tried to force her eyes to stay open, but she blinked. And that quickly, the girl's face was gone.

"So who is it?" Anne asked.

"I don't know," Juniper said, rubbing her eyes. "She's not there anymore."

"It was probably just your reflection," Anne said.

"No, it wasn't." Juniper looked out through the lace curtains that dressed her bedroom window. The late afternoon sun conjured images of iced tea on the back porch, backyard badminton, and swatting mosquitoes. Long shadows stretched across the street. This was a normal summer evening. But Juniper didn't feel normal at all. She shivered.

"Well, who do you think it was?" Anne asked.

"Whoever it was is not important," Gena said. "Did you see my retainer?"

"Forget your retainer!" Anne snapped. She turned back to Juniper. "Why do you think she appeared to you?"

"I don't know," Juniper said, suddenly confused. "It's all so creepy."

"Are you sure it wasn't your reflection?"

"I hardly think so!" Juniper said. All the questions had her dizzy. Her thoughts trickled away like sand through a funnel. "Look, I have dark hair and a dark complexion. This girl had light brown hair, and was as pale as a ghost."

"Well, maybe that's it," Anne said. "If she's a ghost, we could have a séance and summon her here."

"And if I don't find my retainer soon, a séance is the only way you guys'll be able to contact me!" Gena said.

The telephone rang.

Juniper forced a half smile. "Maybe I should look back into the bowl and see if that's Anne's mom or your dad on the phone," she said to Gena.

"It's not my dad. He's working till seven."

Joy Lynch, Juniper's mom, poked her head through the doorway. "Anne, your mom called to say it's time for dinner."

"Thanks," Anne said.

"I should go too," Gena said. "I promised my dad I'd finish cleaning out my closet."

After the girls were gone, Juniper sat on her bed and looked out the window again. She thought of the girl and chills danced down her spine. Was she a ghost? Juniper didn't think so.

The evening shadows had run together by the time her mom called her to dinner.

Juniper usually enjoyed dinner in the summer. It was the only time her family all sat down to-gether and ate. The school year was just too busy. Between her dance classes and her brother Jonathan's Little League, they were usually eat-ing in the car after swinging through the local fast-food drive-in.

Tonight was different though. Juniper picked at her food. Odd thoughts raced through her mind like school kids racing to beat the tardy bell. She couldn't control the images—there, then gone.

"Juniper, did you hear your mother? She asked you a question."

She didn't have to look at her dad's face. She could tell by his voice he wasn't pleased with her.

"Sorry, Mom, what'd you say?"

"I asked if Gena is going to Chicago next week with her father."

"Yeah, but she's not too happy about it," Juniper said as she watched her mom balance a row of peas on her fork. "They'll be there for three days, and she'll be stranded in the hotel room all day while he works. But she said the hotel does have cable, so it won't be a total loss."

Juniper thought about Gena and her retainer, and the face in the water. Maybe she should tell her mom. Her mom would understand. After all, the ladies were always stopping by to sample Joy Lynch's special tea. Actually, it wasn't her tea that was special, it was the goop that settled at the bottom of the cup. Her mom read tea leaves. It was part of that family tradition, passed down from mother to daughter. Things had come full circle, and it was Juniper's time to learn. She sat in on a lot of her mom's tea readings, but the ladies were so boring. They only wanted to know if their husbands were getting a raise, or if they'd be taking a trip.

Juniper decided against telling anyone about the girl she saw in the water. Tomorrow she probably wouldn't even remember what the girl looked like. She went back to picking at her food.

After clearing the dishes, she passed on a family evening of Monopoly and flopped down on the couch instead. She flipped the channels on the TV remote, but every show seemed to be a rerun of a Christmas episode. *Christmas in June just isn't the same,* Juniper thought. She couldn't have felt festive even if it had been December. She turned off the TV and went to her room.

She crawled into bed and looked across at the posters pinned to the wall. This was the same room she'd slept in since they moved here seven years ago, but tonight it was different . . . unfamiliar. She reached for the phone and dialed Gena's number.

"Hello."

"Gena, it's me," Juniper said.

"Are you *crazy?*" Gena whispered. "If my dad finds out I'm on the phone after 10:00, he'll kill me."

"Well, he's going to kill you anyway for losing your retainer. This will be a quicker, less painful death."

"What do you want?" Gena asked.

"It's that girl I saw. Something's not right. I can't stop thinking about her."

"What do you think we should do?" Gena said a little louder this time.

"I don't know, but it felt like she was trying to tell me something. Maybe after we find your retainer, we should investigate some more. It's really bothering me."

Juniper felt better having Gena on the phone. She wished they could talk all night, but she knew that was impossible.

"Do you have any idea who this girl is?" Gena asked.

"No," Juniper said with a chill. "But she really scares me."

CHAPTER 3

The Search

Fighting sleep, Juniper couldn't stop yawning during breakfast. She'd barely slept all night, and the little sleep she did get was a marathon of nightmares. Getting out of bed felt a lot like crawling out of a dark hole.

She leaned over her cereal and looked down at the five soggy Os left floating in the bowl of milk. They appeared to be doing a square dance. *Do-si-do, round and round.* Then, as if drawn by a magnet, they came together in a star shape and settled at the edge of the bowl. *This cereal is trying to tell me something,* she thought.

Just then, Jonathan came into the kitchen dribbling a basketball.

His jersey hung over his shorts, and his bony legs gave him the appearance of a stork.

"You're not supposed to be doing that in the house, you know," she reminded him.

Jonathan shrugged. "So, what was wrong with you last night?"

"Nothing. What are you talking about?" She had enough to worry about without being quizzed by her dopey brother.

"You were yelling in your sleep. You kept waking everybody up. Mom finally went in to check on you because she thought you had a fever or something. So, what was wrong?"

"Nothing," Juniper said, looking down at the formation in her milk.

"Well, something was wrong because you were howling like an old hound dog." Jonathan wiped his sweaty black hair away from his forehead.

"Did you come in here for a reason?" Juniper asked, irritated. She always wondered if Mom had Jonathan just to punish her.

"Oh yeah," Jonathan said, "your goofy friends are out in the front yard waiting for you."

Juniper jumped up, then looked back down at the message in the cereal. *Oh well,* she thought. She scooped it all into the spoon and gulped it down.

Juniper rushed to the front door and flung it open. Anne and Gena sat straddling their bikes.

"You're not dressed yet!" Gena complained.

Juniper looked down at the faded blue T-shirt she had slept in. "Okay, okay, just give me a minute."

She ran to her room, and, in two minutes flat, had squirmed into a pair of blue jean shorts and her favorite green shirt. Brushing her long dark hair took the most time. The ends always knotted up. When the last tangle was free, she threw down the brush and rushed out.

Juniper stood waiting while the garage door cranked open, revealing Anne and Gena on the other side. She walked her bike out on to the driveway.

"Okay," she said, "where are we going to look first?"

"I was on Park Place Drive day before yesterday," Gena said. "I went to pick up some things at FastMart. I could have lost it there."

"How can you possibly lose a retainer at Fast-Mart?" Anne asked.

"I don't know," Gena snapped, "but I had to lose it somewhere. It didn't just run away."

Those last two words stung Juniper like a needle. *Run away.*

It echoed in her ear. She shook it off for the moment and said, "Stop arguing and let's go."

All three girls pushed off at the same time and pedaled down the street.

Park Place Drive was only six blocks away, so it didn't take long for them to get there. Juniper loved the ancient oak trees that spread in the middle of the road, splitting the right and left lanes. But she hated the way people nailed signs and posters to them. It gave the road a trashy look.

"Okay, here's FastMart," Gena said. "Keep your fingers crossed."

Juniper felt a blast of cold air hit her the minute the electronic doors slid open.

"Over there," Gena said, pointing to lane seven. "That's the same lane I used two days ago."

The girls approached a tall, skinny woman at the registers.

"Excuse me, ma'am," Gena said quietly. "I was wondering if you found a retainer in here the other day."

"Huh?" the woman said, giving Gena a strange look.

"A retainer," Gena went on.

"You know," Anne added, "a dental appliance."

"Oh, dental items are on aisle nine," the woman said as she went back to checking groceries.

"No, you don't understand. I think I lost my retainer in here the other day. Did you find it?"

"Nope," the woman said.

Juniper spoke up. "Can we speak to the manager?"

The woman never looked up. With her thumb, she motioned over her shoulder toward the courtesy booth.

"Thanks," Juniper said.

The lady behind the courtesy booth was wearing a sweater. *Why did stores and restaurants always turn their thermostats so low in the summer?* Juniper wondered.

"Can I help you?" the lady asked politely.

Just as Gena opened her mouth, Juniper interrupted. "Do you have a Lost and Found?"

"No, not really. If someone loses a wallet, we dig through it to find out who it belongs to, then we return it. Did you lose a wallet?"

"No," Gena said. "My retainer."

"Sorry, we haven't found anything like that."

"Thanks." Gena turned away, shoulders slumped.

Juniper was glad to step out into the sunshine. She was starting to feel like one of the store's Popsicles. "So, where to now? Did you go anywhere else the other day?"

"Yeah," Gena said, "I went into the Dairy Treat and got a frozen fudge bar."

"Duh!" Anne said jokingly. "Wouldn't that be the most likely place you'd take out your retainer?"

"No!" Gena said, "I ate the bar on my way home." She stuck her tongue out at Anne.

Juniper climbed on to her bike. "So, you could have dropped it while you were riding home, right? Should we be checking the gutters?"

"Let's check Dairy Treat first," Anne said. "I could go for a Coke right about now."

Juniper still felt chilled from the store, but a soda sounded good anyway.

The Dairy Treat was visible from the FastMart. The sign, a large metal ice cream cone with eyes and a smile, always gave Juniper a warm feeling. No Saturday matinee was complete without a trip to the Dairy Treat. It was a family tradition as far back as she could remember.

As they rode up to the parking lot, Juniper's heart sank. "Oh, gross! It's Beth Wilson and Nicole Hoffman. The Snotty Twins!"

"Hi, Anne," Beth called out.

Naturally, Beth and Nicole would talk to Anne. Anne was a cheerleader. Juniper sometimes wondered why Anne even hung out with her and Gena. Not that Anne was snotty too. Anne liked everyone, and everyone liked Anne.

Anne got off her bike and strolled up to Beth and Nicole. Juniper and Gena stayed put. No use inviting insults. Juniper glanced over at Gena.

Gena stared down at her shoelaces and rocked her bike forward and back, forward and back, like she was lost in another world.

Gena would never fit into Beth's crowd. Her reddish blond hair never looked brushed. It hung down in stringy little spikes, sometimes covering her face. Many times at school Juniper braided Gena's hair after gym class, letting Gena think she was doing it just to pass the time.

Juniper had no idea what Anne and the Snotty Twins were talking about, nor did she care. She just wanted those two to leave so the Fortune Tellers Club could get on with the investigation. She was about to say something to Gena when she noticed Beth and Nicole coming toward them. Gena rocked faster.

"Well, if it isn't the fortune teller," Beth said to Juniper, blasting death rays with her eyes.

"Hi, Beth," Juniper said.

"So, tell me, Fortune Teller, have you cast any spells lately?" Beth giggled and Nicole let out a snorty, obnoxious laugh.

"How do you think you got that zit on your nose?" Juniper said, shooting a few death rays back.

The laughter stopped.

"Come on, Nicole," Beth said, turning away. "Let's see if my mom will drive us to the mall."

They avoided Gena like she was the Cootie Queen. But before climbing on their bikes, Nicole called out, "Hey, Gena, lose something?"

Gena's head popped up so fast Juniper thought she'd get whiplash.

The Snotty Twins hopped on their bikes and pedaled away.

Once inside the Dairy Treat, the girls approached the walk-up counter. The employees were no more helpful than the ones at Fast-Mart. Another dead end.

The girls each ordered a Coke and slid into a booth. It was definitely time to rethink things.

Gena sat, sloshing the ice in her drink, and looking like she'd flunked a major exam.

"Can you think of anything else with the word *park*?" Anne asked.

Juniper shrugged. "I'm running out of ideas."

Gena raised her eyes, her face glum. "I think it means I'll be *park*ing my butt at home when my dad grounds me."

Anne sipped through her staw. Her mouth formed a tiny *o*. "We'll find it."

"So," Juniper said, slurping the last of her drink and tossing the cup into the trash, "I guess we start searching the gutters."

"Maybe we should go ahead and try the park," Anne said as they walked to their bikes. "Just because Gena hasn't been there doesn't mean someone couldn't have picked up the retainer and taken it there."

"Let's look along the road first," Gena said. "I probably just dropped it on my way home. And check in the mouths of all stray dogs and cats!"

"Oh, that's just what you need," Anne added. "A retainer with permanent dog breath."

The girls laughed as they pushed off.

They pedaled slowly. Gena and Anne agreed to check the road while Juniper rode as lookout. She figured getting hit by a truck was far worse than losing a retainer.

As they passed the majestic oaks again, Juniper read some of the signs nailed to them. Each poster started with either *LOST* or *FOUND*. Mostly *LOST*. *Maybe we should put up one for Gena's retainer,* she thought. Then Juniper slammed on the brakes. Her bike skidded sideways, causing Gena to smash into her back tire.

"Hey!" Gena complained, "What'd you stop for?"

But Juniper didn't answer. Her throat knotted. She stared straight ahead into the clump of trees.

She had always been open to the supernatural and her ability to see beyond the real world, but at this moment it slapped her in the face.

"What is it?" Anne asked. "Are you okay? You're as white as a poodle!"

Juniper pointed to a poster tacked to a tree. The top simply read *MISSING*, but the photocopied picture stood out like a billboard. Her heart skipped.

"It's her," she said. "It's the girl in the water."

CHAPTER 4

Missing

MISSING
Laurie Simmons
Age: 9
Hair: Light brown
Eyes: Brown
Suspected Runaway

L ast seen on Tuesday, June 16, wearing a yellow shirt
and brown shorts. If you have any information
please contact the Cullen County Sheriff's Department at
555-7770 or call the Center for Missing Children.

"That's her?" Gena asked.

Juniper nodded her head, her trembling hand still pointing at the poster. "I've got to go," she croaked.

She ran six or seven steps holding on to her bike before she remembered to hop on. She pedaled hard, racing toward her house, leaving Anne and Gena by the side of the road.

When Juniper reached her driveway, she didn't bother with the brakes. She dragged the toe of her sneaker on the pavement, then hopped off, letting the bike drop to the ground. She hurried into the cool dark house.

Her mom stood in the kitchen folding laundry as Juniper plopped down in one of the dinette chairs. She folded her arms and laid her head down on the table.

"Juniper Danielle Lynch!" her mom cried. "You have been out riding your bike in the heat of the day again!" Juniper said nothing as her mom hurried to the refrigerator and poured a tall glass of lemonade. "You know better than that. You're just begging for a heat stroke!"

Juniper took small sips as her mom went back to folding clothes. Her brain was as jumbled as a puzzle with missing pieces. Her mom continued to gripe, but Juniper wasn't listening. The only sound she heard was the loud snapping of the kitchen clock. Pop! Pop! Pop! Each tick reminded her that the future was always one second away. After a few more sips of lemonade, she managed to find her voice.

"Mom, did you hear anything about a runaway girl in town? A girl named Laurie Simmons?"

"Yes, awful isn't it?" Mom said.

"Does anyone know where she went?" Juniper was afraid to hear the answer, but she had to know.

"Not yet. The police are searching. I read in the newspaper that she was here visiting her grandmother."

Juniper watched as her mom folded underwear. She draped each pair gently with special talent. Juniper hated the way her mom always called them "delicates." Why couldn't she just say "underwear" like everyone else?

"That girl's parents must really be worried," Juniper said before taking another sip of lemonade.

"That's just it," Mom said. "The news article said that because they're having some marriage problems, the little girl kept threatening to run away. They sent her here temporarily while they worked things out."

Juniper closed her eyes and recalled the face she had seen in the glass. *If that little girl ran away,* she thought, *she ran in the wrong direction.*

"Couldn't you read her tea leaves? You might be able to see where she is."

"I wish I could," her mom answered with a sigh. "But the girl would have to be here to drink the tea, and if she were here, she wouldn't be missing, would she?"

"Good point," Juniper said. She felt silly for asking.

Just then, Jonathan threw open the sliding glass door and came tracking into the kitchen. "Any lemonade left?" he asked, opening the fridge.

Juniper was in no mood for *him*. She slid out of the chair and hurried to her room. She dropped down on her bed so hard, her head bounced on the pillow. She felt numb, lying there, studying the swirling patterns on the ceiling. One circle rolled into the next. It looked like a chain. *Circles again,* Juniper thought.

A few moments later, Juniper heard a knock on the front door. She didn't need a crystal ball to predict who was there. Muffled voices drifted through her bedroom door.

"Hi. Is Juniper okay?" It was Gena.

"You girls just amaze me!"

Uh, oh! Juniper thought. *Here comes Mom's big lecture.*

"I bet it's nearly 100 degrees out there already, and you're out riding bikes! I know you girls are smarter than that. Heat exhaustion is a serious matter!"

Her mom's voice got steadily louder, warning Juniper that they were heading her way. She felt a bit guilty. Maybe pretending to be weak would be a good enough excuse for deserting her friends in such a hurry. The bedroom door slivered open.

"You all right?" Gena asked, smushing her face in the door crack.

"Yeah, come in, silly."

Gena and Anne tiptoed in like someone visiting a hospital patient. Mrs. Lynch stepped in behind them.

"Juniper, you should eat something. I'm going to make you all some sandwiches."

"I'm okay, Mom," Juniper said as her mom left the room.

Anne closed the door. "We read the poster on Park Place Drive," she said. "Is that really the girl you saw in the water yesterday?'

"Yes," Juniper said, sitting up. "It was her."

She thought of the face on the poster and the image in the bowl. It was like a before and after picture. But after what?

"This is freaky," Gena said.

"You're telling me. I don't know what to think. Why would I see her?"

Anne and Gena shook their heads as they sat down on the end of Juniper's bed.

"The police think she ran away," Juniper told them.

"Do you think she's sending you a psychic message?" Anne asked.

"I don't know, but it's really giving me the creeps. If she just ran away, why can't the police find her?"

"Maybe she found a great hiding place," Gena offered.

"But why would she hide?"

"Maybe she wanted attention," Anne said.

"Well, she got it! I won't be able to think about anything else until I find her." Juniper nervously chewed her nails.

"You!" Anne said, pulling Juniper's fingers out of her mouth. She examined the ragged fingernails and gave Juniper a distasteful look.

"This girl is trying to tell me something. I think it's time for the Fortune Tellers Club to go to work."

"Whoa!" Gena held her hand up like a police-man stopping traffic. "You see a girl floating in a bowl of H_2O and suddenly that's more impor-tant than my missing retainer?"

"Well, this is a real matter of life and death!" She couldn't believe Gena could be so selfish.

"You don't know that," Gena argued. "Kids run away every day."

"Don't ask me how I know," Juniper said. "I just know. Now, are you in, or do Anne and I have to figure this out by ourselves?"

Gena narrowed her eyes. "Okay, Sherlock, you're the fortune telling expert, but we're not totally giving up on my retainer."

"So what're we going to do?" Anne asked.

Juniper sprang from the bed. "I'll get the tarot cards."

She shoved aside a stack of board games on a shelf and grabbed a yellow silk draw-string bag. Inside, she dug out a set of *Rider-Waite Tarot* cards. Her favorite kind. Each card contained a colorful illustration. To Juniper, reading tarot cards was like looking at a picture book. Each card told a story.

The girls sat in a circle on Juniper's bed. "Three cards," Juniper said as she shuffled.

Anne looked surprised. "Just three?"

"In this case, anything more than that might get confusing."

Juniper stopped shuffling and turned up the first card. The Moon. "The card of separation," she said, disappointed. "Now tell us something we don't know."

Next, the Strength card came up. "Hmmm . . . the poor kid is really struggling. Or this could mean inner strength." Juniper tried to sound like the expert that Gena and Anne always claimed she was.

"Or it could be physical strength," Anne offered. "Who knows, she could be tied up somewhere."

Gena nodded in agreement.

The thought of that sent a cold shiver through Juniper. "Last card," she said.

The Eight of Wands.

The three girls gazed down at the card like it was written in Chinese.

"What does this look like to you?" Juniper asked.

"A bunch of sticks," Gena said.

Juniper turned the card sideways and studied it. "Now what does it look like?"

"You can't do that," Anne said.

"Why not?" Juniper asked.

"You're supposed to read tarot cards upright or reverse, not sideways."

"They're my cards, I can read them any way I want. So, what do they look like?"

"A bunch of sticks," Gena said.

"No, really."

"Really?" Gena rubbed her chin. "A bunch of sticks."

Juniper's mom appeared with grilled cheese sandwiches, corn chips, and lemonade. She smiled down at the cards.

"Don't you girls know that the future is more exciting if you don't know what's going to happen."

"Look who's talking," Juniper said, reaching for her plate. "Madam Tea Leaves."

They all giggled as Juniper's mom handed them their lunch, then left the room.

"Gena's right," Anne said, covering her mouth as she chewed. "It looks like sticks."

"The woods?" Gena asked.

"It could be a campfire," Anne suggested.

"No, no, no, I think Gena's right," Juniper said. "It represents trees or something." She tried hard to concentrate.

"The lumberyard?" Anne said, weakly.

"Yes!" Juniper shouted, slapping her hand on the floor. She felt they were on to something. "We'll check the old lumberyard. There are a lot of places she could hide there."

"Oh yeah, right," Gena said, rolling her eyes. "Like your mom would actually let us go there. That place is a neglected nightmare. And it's not exactly in Mr. Rogers' neighborhood, if you know what I mean."

"We don't have to tell her. We'll say that we're going swimming at Anne's."

"Wouldn't that be lying?" Gena asked with a crooked grin.

"Not if we really go swimming at Anne's. We'll just . . . take the long way."

"We'll have to stop off at my apartment and get my swimsuit," Gena added.

"No problem. Let's go!"

The three girls raced about like the fast forward on a remote control. Juniper reached into her bottom drawer for her swimsuit.

Anne took a moment to sweep grilled cheese crumbs off Juniper's bedspread with her hand.

Gena grabbed another fistful of corn chips as they stormed out the door.

CHAPTER 5

No Trespassing!

The girls squinted as they rode their bikes under the blistering sun. The heat from the pavement formed mirages ahead—small puddles that vanished as they approached. Juniper thought of the cool water of Anne's swimming pool and loosened her fingers on the heat-softened rubber hand grips.

Third Street. Juniper had a hard time believing that this area was just blocks from her neighborhood. Her parents avoided it like a bad fever blister. "Stay away from there," Mom would say. "That place is full of dope heads and hoodlums." Juniper wasn't sure about that, but she was sure about one thing. It was full of poverty. The rows of shacks leaned so much, Juniper imagined one small sneeze toppling them over. Dirty children played barefoot under a tree. An old man with no teeth grinned at them from a tiny porch with a green awning. The green was mildew. The man waved as they rode by.

Juniper thought a sign should be posted at the street corner. *WARNING! THE USE OF PAINT IS STRICTLY PROHIBITED BEYOND THIS POINT BY ORDER OF THE POVERTY POLICE.*

NO TRESPASSING was the sign that greeted them as they turned into the gravel driveway leading to the abandoned lumberyard. The girls hid their bikes behind some overgrown bushes.

"Okay," Gena said, "how do we get in?"

The wooden privacy fence that surrounded most of the lumberyard looked new and out of place. Juniper pointed to the once-used entrance blocked by four strands of thorny barbed wire. "We go through there."

Stepping on the bottom wire, and pulling up on the third, stretched the fence enough for each girl to take turns slipping through. Anne caught her shorts on one of the barbs, but Juniper carefully popped it loose before it tore the fabric.

"I can't believe people give this place the honor of calling it a lumberyard," Juniper said. It looked more like a disaster. She imagined that it could be cleaned up and turned into a nice park or picnic area, but not unless somebody really cared. Juniper wondered why this whole area was forgotten.

"Not exactly the lovely pine smell you get at Hal Woody's Home Improvement Center, huh?" Gena said.

"Not at all," Anne said. "It's more like a graveyard for old telephone poles and rotten trees."

"Yes," Gena announced a little too loudly, "this is where lumber comes to die!"

"The old folks home for logs," Juniper said. "And chiggers."

She reached down and clawed at her stinging legs. "Let's get out of these weeds."

"Yes," Gena said laughing, "those weeds over there would be much better to stand in."

"The whole place is weeds," Anne said. "Let's hurry up and look for the girl so we can go swimming. I'm about a heartbeat away from a heat stroke."

The girls tip-toed through the overgrown brush, occasionally stopping to pull burrs from their socks.

"You know what would really add to this party, Juniper?" Gena said. "For a really big snake to come slithering up and say hello."

Anne froze.

"Oh come on, Anne," Juniper urged. "Most snakes are more afraid of us than we are of them."

At that moment, something moved in the grass up ahead.

"Okay, guys," Anne said. "This is dangerous. I think we should go—RIGHT NOW!"

"I'm not going until I know that kid is definitely not here." Juniper said.

"LAURIE!" Gena yelled.

Juniper slapped her hand over Gena's mouth.

"Are you crazy? Do you want everyone in the world to know we're snooping around in here?"

"Sorry," Gena said.

From the corner of her eye, Juniper saw something move under a large pile of wood. "Over there," she said.

A stack of logs had taken a tumble. They had rolled off into a great heap that reminded Juniper of a campfire for Paul Bunyan.

"Hello?" Juniper whispered as the girls took tiny steps toward the pile. They hunched together like kids entering a haunted house.

"Laurie, are you hiding under there?" Juniper said softly.

Something moved under the logs.

"There!" Juniper shouted, breaking away from her friends. She took three giant steps forward when a huge field rat popped out from the lumber, baring its sharp teeth.

"It's a jumping . . . rat . . . Chihuahua . . . thing!" Juniper stuttered.

They all screamed.

The girls ran like track stars, jumping hurdles of splintered wood and rusted spikes. The tall weeds brushed Juniper's legs, but chiggers were the least of her problems. Sweat trickled down her face, burning her eyes. She used the hem of her T-shirt to wipe it away. When she could see clearly again, she knew they were in trouble. Old Man Williams stood blocking the entrance. They were trapped with no way out. Suddenly, the rat seemed like a minor thing.

Old Man Williams, as the kids called him, was the spookiest old grump in town. He lived alone in a rundown two-story house next to the lumberyard. The rumors were that he'd killed his wife, once worked as a circus freak, and ate little kids for breakfast. Juniper grew up hearing all the usual urban legends, and Old Man Williams starred in every one. Now, he stood before them in a stained undershirt, grimy cut-off jeans, and a greasy baseball cap.

The girls stopped running and dragged their feet on the gravel driveway.

"Are you kids nuts in the head or sumthin'?" Old Man Williams barked through brown teeth. "Are you too dumb to read? How many signs do they need to put up before you kids get it through your thick skulls that this place is dang'rous!"

The girls had hovered together again, looking at the ground.

"We're sorry," Gena said lamely.

Old Man Williams shook his head as he walked over to a post holding the barbed wire. He lifted it from the ground to make an opening. "Now git out of here and don't come back!"

The girls ran through the open space and grabbed their bikes. Juniper stared straight ahead until they were off Third Street. A few blocks away, she relaxed her pace and let out a deep breath. By the time they reached Anne's house, her face felt blistered and feverish.

★ ★ ★

Juniper thought the swimming pool was the perfect solution. The water cooled off the heat as well as her fear.

"I think I know what happened to that missing girl," Gena said.

"What?" Juniper and Anne asked together.

"Did you see Old Man Williams's gut? Laurie Simmons with a side of fries."

"Oh, you," Juniper said, splashing Gena with water. "At least he let us go!"

All the swimming, chatting, and splashing around felt great, but Juniper's mind still wandered off. At times, she felt all alone, even though Anne and Gena were right beside her. Yesterday the summer stretched out before her, long and lazy. Today she was lost in a fog, unable to find her way back to the person she was.

"What's wrong with her?" Anne mouthed silently to Gena.

Using her index finger, Gena made small circles by her head.

"I'm not crazy," Juniper said, turning to face them.

Anne and Gena both turned a rosy shade of pink.

"So, are we going to the park after this?" Gena asked.

"Why would we go to the park?" Juniper stared curiously at Gena.

"My retainer? It's still missing. We haven't looked in the park yet."

"I thought you said you haven't been to the park," Juniper reminded her.

"Anne said someone might have picked it up and taken it there."

"Not likely," Anne said. "I was just trying to think of something to give you a little hope."

"Are there places to hide at the park?" Juniper asked, her mind still on Laurie Simmons.

"Will you stop it!" Gena yelled. "I wish you'd never looked in that bowl of water. It's like you're possessed or something."

Juniper ignored Gena's ranting. She looked down at the soft ripples of water in the pool. *Here we are,* she thought. *The Fortune Tellers Club standing waist deep in a crystal ball the size of my living room.* She rubbed her hand along the surface as though she were polishing glass. The events at the lumberyard popped into her mind. *Did that happen just an hour ago?* It seemed like ages. The thought of time caused a sudden eagerness, and Juniper didn't want to waste another minute.

"Let's try it again!" The words shot out of her mouth.

"Try what?" Anne said.

"Crystal gazing again. We'll stand in a circle and concentrate on the water between us. Maybe one of us will have a vision."

"The only vision I want is me smiling with a big ol' piece of metal running through my teeth," Gena said, snapping her fingers.

"Come on!" Anne said, nudging Gena's shoulder.

The girls moved in closer at the shallow end. With knees bent, they stood perfectly still.

Juniper gazed at the blue water. Sparkles of sunlight touched it like a constellation touches the night sky. She relaxed her eyelids and cleared her mind. If Laurie Simmons could connect to her, she had to give her every advantage. Her eyes blurred for a moment, then focused. The strange tingling took over, and odd pictures began to appear on the surface. Pictures that made no sense. Large blotches of color, eyes peeking through the crack of a door, the blue and white drinking straws at Dairy Treat toppling to the ground. Juniper felt hypnotized as the images flashed one after another like the slides in a projector. She held her breath. *Tell me. Tell me,* she thought. At that moment, the water exploded like a bomb, and a tidal wave of water splashed Juniper in the face.

Gena and Anne screamed.

Juniper nearly peed in the pool.

CHAPTER 6

Some Inside Information

W hat are you doing, practicing to be man-
nequins at Bloomingdales?" It was Beth
Wilson.

Standing next to her was Nicole Hoffman. She
grabbed her ribs and laughed like it was the fun-
niest joke in the world.

Juniper glared up at the Snotty Twins. Her face
grew hot in spite of the cool water. She looked
down at her feet, and there at the bottom of the
pool lay a large bottle of bronze tanning lotion.

"You scared us to death!" Anne said. She held her nose and went under to retrieve the lotion. When she came up, Juniper saw that she was grinning. "And the next time you want to throw something at us, pick something that belongs to you."

Juniper couldn't believe Anne had invited those two. Or maybe she hadn't. This could be another reason for Beth to fit Anne into her crowd—she had a pool.

"So what did we miss?" Nicole asked.

"Nothing," Anne said quickly.

Juniper knew Anne wasn't about to tell, and she preferred it that way. All members of the Fortune Tellers Club had agreed to keep their activities secret. Anne was better at that than Gena, although Juniper thought Anne did it to keep from being made fun of, not to uphold club rules.

"I'm surprised you're here," Anne said.

"We almost weren't," Nicole explained. "Beth's mom didn't want us to go out by ourselves. She's still freaking out about the missing kid down the street."

"She lives on *your* street?" Juniper asked, surprised.

"Her grandmother lives on the corner," Beth said. "That kid was just visiting."

"Did you ever see her?"

"Of course not! Now stop talking about it. This whole missing kid thing is weirding me out."

Beth and Nicole stepped down into the pool and squatted until the water barely touched their shoulders. A moment later they sprang back up, climbed out, and lay down on large beach towels.

Juniper rolled her eyes at Gena.

Gena curled her lip and shook her head.

"We can't ruin perfectly good swimsuits by getting them too wet," Juniper whispered.

Gena grabbed her mouth to keep from laughing. She accidentally snorted.

Anne stood near the edge of the pool looking down at Beth and Nicole. "Great swimsuits," she complimented. "I love the wild colors. Are they new?"

Juniper bit her lips to hold back a chuckle. It appeared Gena was trying to do the same.

"We got these at the mall yesterday," Beth explained in a squeaky voice. "Go look at our lace cover-ups on the porch."

She talked as if Anne was the only person there. *What nerve,* Juniper thought.

"Okay," Anne said with a huge smile. "And I'll go in and get us something to drink while I'm at it." She bounced away, slamming the back screen door as she went in.

Fashion bikinis with matching lace cover-ups were the last thing Juniper cared about right now. But she noticed Gena looking down at her faded one-piece. Her own swimsuit didn't measure up either.

Nicole rolled over on her tummy and placed her chin on the back of her hand. "So, what have you two been doing this summer?"

Gena slumped down into the water. "Just hanging out," she said.

"Any luck in your search?" Nicole asked.

This caught Juniper by surprise. Which search? Did she know they were trying to find Laurie Simmons?

"What are you, a couple of spies? How did you know about that?" asked Juniper.

"Anne told us," Beth spouted. "I lost my retainer before and never found it."

Juniper let out a deep breath. She figured Anne must have told them yesterday.

"I'll find it," Gena said.

"So," Beth continued. "What exactly were you doing when we came in?"

"Just thinking," Juniper said.

"Well, you must have been thinking hard because it looked like you were having a staredown with the pool."

Anne came out with five plastic cups of lemonade on a tray.

Juniper planned to take a couple of sips then make up an excuse to leave. Sunbathing with the Snotty Twins was not on her list of priorities. Finding Laurie Simmons was.

After suffering through a few minutes of Cheer Squad Camp news and fashion tips, Juniper spoke up. "I have to go, Anne. Gena and I still need to look for her retainer."

Gena set her drink down and hurried out of the pool.

She was just waiting for me to rescue her, Juniper thought.

Anne looked disappointed as Juniper stepped out too. "Don't you need my help? I could go with you."

"Oh no," Juniper said. "You shouldn't leave your friends here. That would be rude."

"Sit back down, Anne," Beth commanded. "They can find it by themselves."

The expression on Anne's face told Juniper that she did not want to sit down. Her eyes pleaded to come with them.

"But I need to go back to your house anyway," Anne fibbed. "I left my earrings there." She gave Juniper a crooked smile.

"Okay, we can take a hint," Beth surrendered. "Maybe we can come back tomorrow."

"I'll call you," Anne said.

Beth and Nicole grabbed their lace cover-ups and walked out the back gate. Once the latch snapped, the three fortune tellers hurried back into the pool.

Juniper finally got the chance to ask. "Did either of you see anything in the water?"

"Just a bunch of spots," Anne said.

"My mind kept wandering," Gena confessed. "I didn't see anything."

They both looked at Juniper. "Did you see something again?" Anne asked excitedly.

"I saw a lot of things," Juniper explained, "but most of it didn't make sense. I'm sure it had something to do with Laurie Simmons."

"Here we go again!" Gena said, falling backward in the water.

Juniper persisted. "Do either of you have any new ideas?"

"I'm all out," Gena said.

Anne shrugged, then thoughtfully narrowed her eyes. "Have you ever heard of *psychometry*?"

"No, but I think I'm about to," Gena said.

"It's when you touch an object that belongs to someone, and you pick up their vibrations from it. Psychics do it all the time to help the police solve murders and stuff."

"Anne, that's a great idea!" Juniper said.

Gena laughed. "Yeah, I can't believe *you* thought of it. Juniper's our psychic expert, remember?"

Juniper rolled her eyes at Gena even though she too was surprised by Anne's suggestion. "Maybe if one of us held something that belonged to Laurie Simmons, we could figure out where she is."

"And if you grab hold of my teeth, maybe you could find my retainer," Gena said, laughing.

"Get serious," Anne said. She looked at Juniper. "Psychometry could work, but there's one problem. Where are we going to find something that belongs to Laurie Simmons?"

Gena laughed again. "Maybe we can stare in the water and figure that out too!"

"Stop it!" Juniper said to Gena. "This is going to take some detective work, but I think if we go to her grandmother's house we might find something."

"Yeah, right," Gena said. "We'll knock on the door, flash our business cards, and tell Grandma to hand over a toy for us to feel."

"Or we might find something of hers lying in the yard." Juniper said. "We should go over there and check."

Anne and Gena gave each other a doubtful look. "How will we know which house is hers?"

Juniper smiled, thinking of the unwanted visit from Beth and Nicole. *Everything happens for a reason,* she thought.

"I'm sure there's only four corners on Beth's street," Juniper said. "I bet we'll be able to tell which is the right house."

"I hope so," Gena added, "or we'll be accidentally locating some kid who's just off at summer camp."

CHAPTER 7

Something to Hold On To

The house on the corner of Pine and Talbot looked more like an election headquarters than a residence. Yellow ribbons fluttered from the trees. Signs saying *"Laurie, Come Home"* and *"Laurie, We Miss You"* lined the yard. A small patio table held a dozen burning jar candles. A dozen more glowed below it on the porch. Vehicles crowded the street like a used car lot. Three police officers stood talking at the end of the driveway. One rested his foot on the bumper of his patrol car.

"Yep," Gena said, "this ought to be easy."

This was not the scene Juniper had expected. Somehow she'd thought the place would be more like a funeral parlor.

"So what do we do now?" Anne asked.

Juniper stood staring at the cluttered yard. No Barbie doll, no stuffed animal, no story-book—nothing that looked like it would belong to Laurie Simmons. And even if one of those things had been there, how would she explain taking it?

Anne and Gena looked at Juniper as though they were waiting for an answer.

"Juniper," Gena said a bit nervously, "please tell me you're not planning to knock on this lady's front door."

"No. Let's go around and look at the back."

"Juniper," Gena said, weaving her bike in and out of parked cars, "please tell me you're not planning to knock on this lady's back door."

"Oh hush!" Anne said.

Juniper noticed one of the policemen watching them. He took a couple of steps in their direction then stopped and turned back to the other officers.

Juniper held her breath until they were well behind the back privacy fence and invisible to the cops.

"This is hopeless," Anne said. "Not to mention dangerous. What if we get caught?"

"We won't get caught," Juniper assured her. "Hold my bike against the fence so I can step up on it and look over."

"She's crazy," Gena said to Anne. "You're crazy," she said to Juniper.

"Just hold the bike!"

Juniper grabbed the handlebars and put her foot up on the seat of her bike. Thank goodness for long legs. She boosted herself up and flung her leg back as if she were performing at one of her dance recitals. Taking hold of the fence, she slowly inched her way up and peeped over the top.

Before her eyes could focus on the view of the backyard, the biggest dog with the sharpest fangs in canine history leapt up and snarled in Juniper's face. A string of dog slobber hit her chin as she toppled backward and landed on her bottom.

"Are you okay?" Gena asked as she and Anne pulled Juniper back to her feet.

"I was until the Wolfman appeared," Juniper said, wiping her chin with the sleeve of her shirt. "Anybody have a silver bullet?"

"Oh wait here, I'll just run and ask one of the nice officers in the front," Gena said.

"Any suggestions on how to handle this?" Juniper asked.

"Yeah," Anne said, "we go home."

"Any other suggestions?"

"I know. Let's distract that puppy." Gena began unscrewing the twist tie on a garbage bag leaning against the back corner of the fence. "There's got to be a nice doggy treat in here somewhere."

The smell that wafted up from the bag told Juniper that this trash had missed its ride on trash day.

"Whoa!" Gena leaned back, holding her nose and fanning her face.

"Nice odor," Anne said, leaning against the fence.

Juniper, who had knelt down by Gena, smiled up at Anne. "It smells like Gena's locker."

Gena slapped Juniper's shoulder with the back of her hand. They all giggled.

Juniper could hear the dog panting on the other side of the fence.

"Okay," Gena said, rummaging through the trash again. "What do we have in here for the poochie-woochie?"

Right away Gena brought up a chicken bone with a few pieces of gristly meat hanging limply from it. "This ought to do it," she said. She held it at arms length like it was nuclear waste.

As they tiptoed back to the bike, Juniper could hear the dog on the other side of the fence, following them like a magnet.

Just as Juniper pulled herself up on her bike, Gena flung the chicken leg over the fence as hard as she could. The sound of paws zipping through the grass told Juniper all was clear for a moment. She peeped over the fence again.

The dog, which now appeared three sizes smaller, sat near a tree gnawing on his prize. The backyard looked like a foreign country compared to the front. The grass needed mowing, but other than that, the area was empty except for a couple of lawn chairs.

Juniper could see a lot of backyards from where she stood. And beyond them, she could see the lumberyard and the water tower. Suddenly, looking for Laurie seemed like looking for a flea on the dog gnawing his chicken bone.

"What do you see?" Anne asked.

"No use," Juniper said as she climbed down from her bike. "There's nothing back here either."

"Thank goodness," Anne said. "I'd hate to think what genius idea you'd come up with to get us in there if you'd found something."

"It's not fair!" Juniper griped. "I know if I had something of hers I could help."

"Would you like to tell that to the three large police officers in the front yard who may still come walking back here any minute?" Anne asked.

"Yeah, losing my retainer *and* being brought home in a squad car is not the best Father's Day present I can think of," Gena added.

The girls walked their bikes between a couple of cars parked on the grass. Gena stopped suddenly as they came to the road. "Wait! When someone stays at your house, not all the trash is yours, right? So some of that trash over there must be Laurie Simmons."

"Ewwwwww," Anne said, making a sour face. "We're not digging through that garbage again!"

"Yes we are," Juniper said.

They turned their bikes around and went back to the fence.

The trash bag was still open, and now some flies were swarming over it.

"Oh great," Juniper said, "this time we have visitors."

She waved her hand over the bag to shoo the flies away, but then remembered that's why they are called pests, they don't leave.

Juniper opened the bag wide and a couple of nasty items fell out. A paper towel soaked in bacon grease, and a can half full of moldy bean dip.

Gena kicked them out of the way.

"Litter bug," Anne said.

Juniper thought about how the bag was over-stuffed. Overstuffing the trash bag was some-thing her mom constantly yelled at her and Jonathan about. But at least this one did start out with a twist tie when they arrived. Something impossible to achieve with their trash at home.

"How are you going to know which trash is hers?" Anne asked.

"Good question. I'll just have to try and fig-ure it out."

"I know, why don't you pick up every single piece of garbage in there and feel for the vibes?" Gena giggled.

"Oh, shut up!" Anne said, also giggling.

Juniper didn't feel like giggling. The heat of the afternoon and the smell of the trash were making her stomach churn like an old washing machine. *I won't throw up!* she thought as she rummaged through bottles and cans and bits of food. The flies had doubled and were on the attack.

Pushing her way to the bottom, Juniper also wondered how she would know which trash was

Laurie's. Maybe she would get lucky and find a candy wrapper. A "kids only" candy like Sour Bombs that no self-respecting grandma would put in her mouth. The thought of sour candy made Juniper's mouth pucker and her stomach turn over. *I won't throw up!* She brushed away more flies.

Juniper choked and gagged a couple of times as she pushed more garbage out of the way. Then she saw something that gave her hope. A half-eaten hamburger and a small bag with a couple of french fries lay near the bottom.

"This is it," she said, carefully taking hold of a paper cup decorated with monkeys and elephants.

"How do you know it's hers?" Gena asked.

Juniper stood up, away from the flies and the rotten smell. "Do you think Grandma ate a Circus Meal from Jumbo Burger?"

Gena looked down again at the tiny cup Juniper was holding by the rim.

"Thank goodness," Anne said, letting out a deep breath. "Now let's get out of here."

Juniper was a bit unsteady as she walked to her bike. She still felt sick. Her only thought now was getting home and lying on her cool bed.

The girls grabbed their bikes and threaded through the maze of cars again when someone shouted behind them.

"Hey! What are you doing back there?"

CHAPTER 8

The Trance

The girls froze. Gena's hands flew up as though she were under arrest. Her bike went crashing to the ground.

Big trouble! Juniper thought as she slowly looked back.

The girls turned around in slow motion.

Instead of a giant, burly cop with a badge the size of a lunch plate, they saw a short, skinny man who looked like he'd slept in his clothes. A clump of hair drooped down on his forehead and his scraggly mustache hid his top lip.

"Why are you fooling around back here?" This time his question didn't seem as threatening.

After a long silence, Anne spoke up. "We're sorry. It's just that we lost something and we were riding around the neighborhood looking for it."

"What did you lose?" the wimpy, little man asked, cocking an eyebrow and giving them a suspicious stare.

"I lost my retainer," Gena said. "If I don't find it, I'm in big trouble."

The man looked at Gena with tired eyes. "I lost something too," he said. "Something valuable." He glanced away, then raised his eyes to the sky, fighting back tears.

Familiar eyes, Juniper thought. *Laurie Simmons's eyes.* She had no doubt they were facing Laurie's father.

"We're sorry," Anne said again, a little softer.

Mr. Simmons crammed his hands deep into the pockets of his wrinkled pants. "Well, you girls better get home. It's not safe for kids your age to be out running around."

Without hesitation, the three of them turned back to their bikes. Gena stumbled trying to pick hers up off the ground.

Juniper looked at the paper cup she still held, pinched between her thumb and index finger. She felt her lunch rising to her throat again and swallowed hard to keep it down.

As they were ready to ride off, the man yelled, "Wait!"

The girls stopped and turned around.

"Where would you go if you ran away?" the man asked with a shaky voice.

Juniper would never forget the look of desperation on his face. "Probably some place the police have already looked," she said.

Mr. Simmons nodded his head slightly, then shuffled slowly back to the house like a whipped dog.

★ ★ ★

Juniper sat down at her kitchen table while Anne drew a glass of water.

"Remember," she said, handing the glass to Juniper, "this is to drink, not to stare in."

Juniper gulped it like someone stranded in the desert.

She set the glass on the table next to the paper cup from Jumbo Burger.

Gena filled glasses of water for Anne and herself. "Can this day get any better? A rat, a crazy old man, rummaging through garbage?"

Juniper looked at the paper cup. Her hands trembled. "Once I get my strength back, we can get to work."

"To work!" Gena said, slamming her hand on the table. "Look at you! I don't know if you're obsessed or possessed, but I can tell you're sick, so you need to take it easy. Laurie Simmons and fortune telling can wait."

"I'm okay," Juniper said weakly.

"You're not okay," Anne said. "For once in her life, Gena's right."

"Hey!" Gena shot back.

Anne shrugged.

"I'm okay!" Juniper insisted. "Now let's go to my room and do this."

"You know what?" Anne said, rising from her chair, "I just remembered why you're my friend. You're crazy!"

"You got that right," Gena said, scraping her chair across the floor.

As Juniper gently picked up the paper cup, another wave of nausea hit her. She stumbled to her bedroom and sank down on the carpet, her back against the foot of her bed. When she put the cup down on the floor in front of her, her stomach relaxed.

"It's the cup," Juniper told her friends. "It's the cup that's making me sick, not the smell from the garbage."

"Yeah, well, hauling around someone's used drink cup kind of makes me sick too," Gena said.

Anne cocked her head and raised her eyebrows. "I don't think that's what she means. It's psychometry, right?"

Juniper wilted a bit. "I'm picking up Laurie's feelings just by touching her cup."

"Is she sick?" Anne asked.

"Sick, tired, weak," Juniper said in a whisper. She reached for the cup then pulled her hand away. Maybe the girls were right. Was it really worth it? What if Laurie Simmons had some horrible disease? Juniper wondered what risks she might be taking. A thousand disturbing thoughts ran through her head, but she reached for the cup anyway.

She grinned nervously at Anne and Gena. "It's just a cup, right?"

"A kid's cup," Anne added, "with a monkey, and a lion, and an elephant parading around it. How bad can it be?"

"Yeah," Gena said. "It's a cup from a Circus Meal. Only happy children eat Circus Meals."

Juniper wished she could believe what Anne and Gena were saying. "Oh, this is silly," she said. She snatched the cup into her hand, holding it fully for the first time. Then she fell over as though someone knocked her down. Her right shoulder hit hard against the floor.

"Are you all right?" Anne shouted, reaching to help Juniper up.

Juniper lay still, her left leg twitching, the cup crushed against her chest.

"Get up, Juniper!" Gena pleaded.

Both girls tried lifting her, but Juniper felt plastered to the floor, like someone trapped in a coffin.

"Juniper!" Gena shouted again. "Get up!"

"We can't move," Juniper said, her voice raspy and dry. "We're stuck."

"You're not stuck," Gena said, trying to grab the cup from Juniper's iron-tight grasp.

"Wait!" Anne said, pushing Gena back. "You said, 'We're stuck.' We who?"

"Laurie and I. We can't move."

"Where are you? Where's Laurie?" Anne pressed.

"It's so dark down here," Juniper whimpered. "I'm hot. I'm thirsty. I want to go home."

Juniper began to cry, clutching the paper cup like it was her favorite teddy bear.

"This isn't fun anymore," Gena said, reaching for the cup again.

Anne pushed her hand away.

"Laurie, where are you?" Anne insisted.

"I'm under here! Help me! My leg hurts so bad." Juniper's leg twitched again. "I can't breathe. Please come and get me."

"Where?" Anne shouted. "Where are you?"

Gena yanked the cup from Juniper's hands and flung it across the room.

Juniper relaxed on to the floor like a glob of jelly.

"What did you do that for?" Anne shouted at Gena. "Now we'll never know where Laurie is."

"I don't get it!" Gena shouted back. "Ten minutes ago you called Juniper your friend, and yet you'd let her go through this? You're both weirding me out!"

Juniper sat up, rubbing her leg. "I feel like I was run over by a bus."

"Maybe you were," Anne said with a smile. "Do you remember any of it?"

Juniper switched from rubbing her leg to rubbing her head. "Let's just say I wasn't myself."

"You were there," Anne said. "You must know where Laurie is."

"She's trapped. Tied down or held down somehow. And she's sick."

"Where?" Gena asked.

Juniper closed her eyes and slumped back against her bed. "I don't know. But if she's not found soon, she's not going to make it."

CHAPTER 9

Restless

Sleep came in bits and pieces for Juniper that night. Her bed felt empty and lonely. It was nearly daylight before real sleep came. Disturbing sleep. Nightmares.

Juniper rushed through the crowded hall of her school.

What's the combination? she thought, as she whirled the dial on her locker. If she could just get it open, Laurie Simmons would be there, hiding behind her history book. A history book would be the safest place to hide. Everything in it had already happened. No surprises. No choices.

Right-left-right. Juniper fumbled with the lock, her fingers as slippery as a fish. I'm running out of time, she thought. Running out of time—running out of—running out—running. Juniper ran. She burst into Mr. Gaitlin's history class, where the other kids were already taking a test.

"You're late!" Mr. Gaitlin barked, pointing a fat finger at Juniper. "It's important to be punctual when taking an exam, catching a bus, and looking for missing children. Is that understood?"

Juniper nodded her head at the dream-warped Mr. Gaitlin. She reached for a pencil on his desk and spilled the entire pencil cup. The slim, yellow rods hit the floor and bounced like raindrops in a puddle.

"Will you hurry?" Mr. Gaitlin said through clenched teeth. "You're running out of time."

Juniper stared at the heap of pencils on the floor. The pattern they made looked so familiar. The vision of the toppled straws she had seen in Anne's pool came back to her. This must mean something. She reached down to pick up a pencil when something moved beneath the pile. She kicked the pencils hard and a large, ugly cockroach ran out and scurried across her foot. She covered her mouth to muffle a scream. The roach ran under Mr. Gaitlin's desk. When Juniper looked up again, her teacher was gone. In his place sat Old Man Williams. His crusty baseball cap said TIMBER WOLVES.

"Are you crazy in the head or sumpthin'?" he spat through rotting teeth.

Juniper snatched an exam paper off the desk and had a seat. She turned the paper over to find it was not an exam at all. It was a MISSING poster. The face of Laurie Simmons peered up at her through swollen eyes. Juniper didn't know if they were puffy from pain or tears. Probably both. Below the photo, a picture of an hourglass showed only a few grains of sand left.

Juniper sprang from her chair and dashed past a class full of faceless students. She burst through the door and into her own kitchen. Her brother, Jonathan, was pouring a bowl of cereal. Juniper noticed the brand. Time Cereal—For Energy That Lasts Around the Clock. The back of the box advertised a contest. Find the missing pieces to the puzzle and win a relaxing summer.

Jonathan set the cereal box on the table. "Mom," he shouted, "when you go to the grocery store don't forget, we're almost out of Time." Then Jonathan splashed milk over the flakes. Laurie Simmons' photograph stared up at Juniper from the back of the milk carton. And Juniper couldn't take her eyes off the picture. The room was as silent as a graveyard. Except for the clock. The loud popping of the second hand warned Juniper again.

Juniper woke up in a puddle of sweat. Daylight shone through the lace curtains, making spider-web shadows on the bed. When she tried rolling over, a throbbing ache numbed her leg.

Juniper thought about the weird nightmare and the confusing images. She refused to look at her bedside clock. She didn't care what time it was. Then she thought of a poem she had learned in school.

As I was walking down the stair,
I met a man who wasn't there.

He wasn't there again today.
I wish, I wish, he'd go away.

Juniper wished Laurie Simmons would go away.
Or come back. Either way, she would be free from
the little girl hiding in her mind. Things would be
normal and she could have a relaxing summer.
But Juniper knew winning that prize meant finding the missing pieces, and she was running out
of time.

★ ★ ★

The phone rang three times before Gena
picked it up.

"What are you doing?" Juniper asked.

She heard Gena draw in a deep breath. "Cleaning out my closet."

"I thought you had finished that the other day."

"So did I!" Gena exclaimed. "But my dad's
idea of cleaning a closet is a lot different from
mine. Can you believe he wants me to throw
away a perfectly good pair of jeans just because

they have a hole in the seat? What century is the man living in anyway?"

"So when will you be finished? I could use some company."

"I don't know. I've been holding on to these jeans for twenty minutes. I just can't part with them. Besides, I earned this hole from squirming in my chair fifty minutes a day in Mr. Gaitlin's boring history class. Mr. Gaitlin had a way of helping you forget the Alamo."

"Mr. Gaitlin, what a nightmare." Juniper meant every word.

"Anyway, I have three more pairs just like these I'll have to say good-bye to. That could take a while."

"Maybe I could come over and help you with your tearful farewells."

"My dad won't allow me to have company when I have work to do."

"Well, maybe when he gets home he'll let you come spend the night."

"I'm sure he will, but I'll only come on one condition."

"And what would that be?" Juniper asked a bit defensively.

"That the Fortune Tellers Club spends most of the time trying to psychically locate my retainer! I don't know how much longer I can hide my teeth from my dad. He's bound to find out soon."

"It's a deal," Juniper agreed. "I'll call Anne and see if she can spend the night too."

Juniper felt better after talking to Gena. Tonight would be a special meeting of the Fortune Tellers Club. She would find Gena's retainer even if it drained every ounce of psychic power from her body.

She picked up the phone again and dialed Anne's number.

"Hi, Mrs. Donovan," Juniper said. "Can I talk to Anne?"

"She's not here, Juniper. She went to the movies with Beth Wilson."

Juniper felt a stabbing pain in her heart. She sat a moment, not knowing what to say. Her face burned. "Tell her to call me when she comes in."

The minute the words escaped her mouth, Juniper could have kicked herself for saying them. She didn't want Anne to call. In fact, she never wanted to speak to her again.

"I sure will," Mrs. Donovan said.

Juniper heard the phone go dead, but she still held the receiver in her hand. Traitor—snake—weasel—slime. How could Anne do that to her? How could she be her friend one minute, then hang out with her enemy the next? Juniper wondered if Anne was just with half the Snotty Twins, or if Nicole was there to complete the set. And if Nicole was not there, did that make Beth a traitor too? A snake, a weasel, slime? Oh, she was all those things, with or without Nicole.

Juniper spent the rest of the afternoon on the couch. Staring at a daytime drama on TV, she could identify with the problems the Soap Opera Queen faced. She had been betrayed. Gena had thrown her over for some jeans with a hole in the seat. Anne had thrown her over for a girl with a hole in her head. Not much difference.

Juniper crushed a small throw pillow to her face, burying her hurt, disappointment, and loneliness. The sounds of the soap opera shrank farther away as she cried herself to sleep.

CHAPTER 10

Famished

The sound of voices drifted from the kitchen. Juniper stirred from her nap.

"I'm sorry, Kathy, I just don't see him getting that bonus."

Once the fog cleared in her mind, Juniper realized it was still Friday afternoon. "Kathy" would be their neighbor, Kathy Layton. She was here for her weekly tea reading. "Him" would be her husband, Wesley.

"I do, however, see you having an unexpected guest," her mom continued.

"So I guess I should give up and tell Wesley to go ahead and schedule his two-week vacation," Kathy Layton said with a hint of disappointment. "I was counting on that bonus to help pay for our trip."

Juniper sat up. A dull pain ran from her head to her leg, and her stomach screamed for food. She hobbled into the kitchen where she saw Jonathan leaning against the sink with a bag of mini marshmallows. Juniper plucked the bag from his hands and dumped about six of them into her mouth.

"Hey!" Jonathan snapped with a surprised look.

"Get over it," Juniper said.

"Take it easy, you two," her mom warned, studying the tea cup in front of her. "Don't fill up on marshmallows. Dad's gone on a fishing trip so we're eating out tonight."

"Mexican food?" Juniper asked through a mouthful of white goo.

"If you want," her mom said with a smile.

Juniper couldn't wait to dig into the salsa, two chips at a time.

"I just hope we don't have to sit too close to the mariachi band," Jonathan complained. "Last time they were so loud I couldn't hear myself eating."

"That's why we sat next to them," Juniper said. "So *we* wouldn't have to hear you eat!"

Jonathan stuck his tongue out at Juniper, who pretended to ignore him.

"Mexican food sounds good," Mrs. Layton said.

"Why don't you dump Wesley tonight and come with us?" Mom teased.

"No, no," Mrs. Layton said. "If I'm going to have that unexpected guest you predicted, I need to stay home and clean house."

Juniper limped by them on her way out of the kitchen.

"What's wrong with your leg?" Mom asked.

"Nothing," Juniper fibbed. "It fell asleep while I was lying on the couch."

Jonathan couldn't resist following Juniper and annoying her with a song—"What's that sticking in your skin? Needles, tacks, nails, and pins. Ripping, tearing, out and in. Hope you like the looney bin!"

Just then, the telephone rang. "Saved by the bell," she said, shoving her brother out of the way. "Now go to your room and grow up!"

"Hello," Juniper said.

"Don't hang up! Just hear me out." Juniper had never heard Anne sound so desperate.

"I can't talk right now, Anne," Juniper said, her voice cold. "We're leaving. We're going out to eat, then Gena's coming to spend the night."

"You won't even let me explain? Oh, some friend you are!"

"Me?" Juniper shouted into the phone. "You're the one who went sneaking off with Beth Wilson! What kind of a friend does that make you? A sneaky one!"

"I didn't sneak anywhere," Anne said, defending herself. "I have cheerleading camp in two weeks, so this morning I went to Victory Dance and Cheer Supply to get fitted for my uniform. Beth was there getting measured for hers too. We started talking and she asked if I wanted to go with her to see a movie. We went to see *Love Letters.* You said yourself that you thought the previews were dumb and you didn't want to see it, so I went. It was just the two of us."

Silence. Juniper wasn't sure what to say. She still felt betrayed, forgotten, and lost. Why couldn't Anne see what this was doing to her?

"So you just go off to the movies without thinking about me and Gena and all the problems?"

"Which problems?" Anne asked. "The problem Gena is having or the one you created?"

"Forget it, Anne! Just go off with your cheerleader friends and forget us. Gena and I can take care of this ourselves."

Juniper's voice cracked and her breath grew ragged. She didn't want Anne to hear her cry. She wished she could turn back the clock—go back to the way things were before this psychic fever burned inside her.

"Come on, Juniper, I have to spend an entire week with Beth at cheer camp so I might as well be nice."

As much as she hated to admit it, Anne did have a point. And she was feeling too weak to argue.

"Juniper?"

"Yeah, okay. Do you want to come and spend the night? We can try to concentrate on finding Gena's retainer."

"All right," Anne said, sounding relieved.

"I'm not sure how long we'll be at the restaurant, but we should be home before 8:30. Call Gena and see if she can ride her bike over with you."

"Thank goodness for daylight savings time," Anne said. "See you then."

★ ★ ★

The first thing that greeted Juniper on the restaurant door was a picture of Laurie Simmons. Below the picture were the words *"Have you seen this child? Missing for 3 days now."* Someone had marked through the "3" with a black marker and replaced it with a "4."

Juniper ran her fingers over the picture. *Four days!* If the girl had simply run away, someone would have found her by now. Suddenly, Juniper's throat went dry. She had never been so thirsty. She hurried into the restaurant and drummed her fingers on the table until the waiter brought her a large glass of water. She gulped it.

Her mom and Jonathan stared across at her in amazement.

"Wow," Jonathan said, "if you're that thirsty now, you'll drain the faucets when the tortilla chips get here."

Juniper rolled her eyes. "Why didn't you send him off fishing too?" she asked her mom. "I'm sure Dad could've used the extra bait."

"Maybe *you* should've gone," Jonathan said, spitting the words at her. "Dad needs a new anchor!"

"Be nice," Mom said, glaring over her menu.

Juniper picked up her menu to block her view of Jonathan. She didn't need to read it. She ordered the same thing every time, cheese enchiladas with extra rice, no beans.

Juniper looked back at the picture taped to the glass door. The sun shone through and she could see the outline of Laurie's face in reverse. It looked much different from this angle. Dark lines and shadows made her look old, haggard, lifeless. Juniper quickly turned back. She was struck with an odd feeling. Looking at that picture was like looking in a mirror.

★ ★ ★

8:43. Juniper was just lifting the telephone receiver when Anne rang the doorbell.

"What happened? You were supposed to be here at 8:30."

Juniper looked out the front door when she realized Anne was alone. "Where's Gena?"

"She's grounded," Anne said.

"Grounded! Didn't she get her closet cleaned out?"

"It's not that," Anne explained. "Her dad found out about her retainer. He's hot!"

Juniper leaned back against the front door as she closed it. "It's my fault. I should have concentrated more on finding it. I hope she's not mad at me."

"You know Gena," Anne said. "I bet she'll be grounded for a few days, her dad will buy her a new retainer, and things will get back to normal."

"Still," Juniper said, "I think we should work on finding the one she lost."

Anne followed Juniper into the kitchen. "Can you believe this?" Juniper said. "I ate two enchiladas, a bowl of rice, chips and salsa with queso, and I'm still hungry!"

Juniper grabbed a bag of pretzel sticks from the pantry. As she passed by the refrigerator, she reached in for some Cokes.

"Let's put on some mood music," Anne suggested, once they settled in Juniper's room.

Juniper reached for a cardboard box labeled "New Age Music." She fingered through the few cassette tapes inside. *Tibetan Bells, Gregorian Chants, Ocean Waves, Rain Forest.* But the plastic case holding *Celtic Visions* felt warm to her touch, a message to Juniper that this was the one.

After slipping the cassette into its proper slot, Juniper waited through the silence of the lead tape, hopeful that the music would instantly fill her with foresight. But instead of the reverent drones of ancient druids, the music was upbeat, quick, and lively.

"You call *that* mood music?" Anne asked with a giggle.

"I don't know whether to meditate or dance a jig," Juniper said. She snapped the stop button. "Let's just spread the tarot cards."

She shuffled them carefully, then gently turned up the first card. The Eight of Swords. The picture showed a woman with her arms bound by strips of cloth, her eyes blindfolded. Eight swords stabbed the ground, encircling her like a cage.

"That's Gena all right," Anne said. "I don't think you could pick a better card for being grounded."

Is this how Gena felt? Juniper wondered. *Tied down, unable to move. Blind to what will happen in the future?*

As she reached for her Coke, she hit the bag of pretzels. A pile of pretzel sticks came tumbling down on top of the card. Juniper stopped dead still, her heart racing in her chest. "Oh my gosh!" she yelled in a panic. "She is at the lumberyard!"

"Gena's at the lumberyard?" Anne asked.

"No," Juniper said, jumping to her feet. "This card doesn't represent Gena. That's Laurie Simmons!"

CHAPTER 11

Sneaking Out

After pulling a pair of socks out of a drawer, Juniper leaned into her closet and grabbed her sneakers.

Anne stood up, looking confused. "What do you think you're doing?"

"What does it look like I'm doing?" Juniper said, bunching up one of the socks on her hand and slipping it over her toes.

"You're not going out there!" Anne demanded.

"Hush! You want to let the whole neighborhood in on this?"

"Juniper, are you nuts?"

"Yes," Juniper said, looking up at Anne sadly. "I'm nuts for not going back there sooner."

"And what's your mom going to say?" Anne was trying to keep control.

"I can't think about that right now," Juniper said.

Anne leaned in, nose to nose with her. "Then think about this. It's dark outside and the lumberyard is blocks away."

"I don't have time for this." Juniper pushed Anne's face out of her way and stood up. "Are you coming with me?"

"You are nuts! Juniper, why don't you just tell the police?"

"I'm not even thirteen years old yet. Do you think they would believe me? Besides, I don't have any proof to give them."

"Exactly!" Anne argued. "You have no proof."

Juniper grabbed her backpack from the closet.

"This is insane!" Anne continued.

"I'm telling you, I saw something move under those boards yesterday."

"Right," Anne said. "Ratzilla! Don't you remember, he came charging at us full force."

"I saw something move on the other side of the rat's nest," Juniper insisted.

"Then think about what else is hiding out there. Snakes and scorpions and, oh yes," Anne pointed to the red polka dots on her legs, "chiggers!"

"Good thinking! I should put on some jeans." She hurried about her business, ignoring Anne's pleas.

They tiptoed out of her bedroom and slipped past her mom, who sat in the living room watching the ten o'clock news. When the coast was clear, they exited through the kitchen into the garage.

"Juniper, did you hear anything I just said?" Anne asked, sounding defeated.

"Just when you reminded me there were chiggers." Juniper rummaged for a flashlight.

Luckily, she found one in her dad's toolbox. She'd been afraid he might have taken it with him on his fishing trip. She turned back to Anne one last time. "Are you going with me or not?"

Anne was trembling. "You don't know what's waiting for us out there."

"Yes I do," Juniper said confidently. "Her name is Laurie."

★ ★ ★

Although it was after ten, the streets were filled with traffic.

Friday night, Juniper thought. *Parties, dating, card games. Friday night doesn't close until after midnight.*

A cool breeze blew her hair as they sailed on their bikes, and the full moon provided plenty of light. *Too much light,* Juniper worried. She didn't want anyone to spot them.

They hid their bikes behind the bushes, and this time, Juniper knew how to open the gate. But she had left her confidence back at the house, and her hands were shaking when she tried lifting the post from the ground.

"I'm not going in," Anne informed her as she laid the post down.

"Well, at least step over here and hide behind the wall."

The bright moonlight gave a clear view of the avalanche of lumber piled in the back corner.

"Over there," Juniper said, pointing. "That's where I saw movement."

"Well, get this over with," Anne urged. "I'm so scared I'm about to faint."

Juniper sucked in a chest full of air and walked briskly toward the lumber heap. Something howled nearby. Something with sharp teeth, Juniper supposed. She froze.

"Hurry!" Anne said in a loud whisper. "I think it's just a dog."

Juniper walked faster.

As she approached the pile of boards, she tried peeking through the cracks. "Laurie?" she said in a low voice. "Laurie, are you under there?" She thought she saw something move under the wood. Startled, she gasped, sucking in too much air that burned her lungs. Then gathering courage, she jogged closer to the fallen wood.

She stepped on some stray boards buried in the weeds. A few times they tilted, almost making her lose her balance.

When she reached the giant lumber heap, Juniper carefully stepped up on the boards with her left foot to test their sturdiness. When she repeated this with her right, a searing flame of pain shot up through her leg, almost crippling her.

"Sssssss," Juniper hissed, lifting her foot off the ground. The board came up too. She had stepped on a nail.

She knelt down and untied the laces on her sneaker.

"What's wrong?" Anne called out.

Juniper didn't answer. She pressed the palms of her hands on each side of the board and pushed as hard as she could. She practically bit her bottom lip off to keep from screaming in pain. Burning foam erupted like a volcano from her belly to her throat, but Juniper choked it back down. The nail slowly slid out of her foot, bringing her sneaker off with it. The bottom of her white sock was already stained red. Juniper removed the sock to examine the wound in the bottom of her foot. The flesh was ragged, and blood gushed from it in small pulsing beats.

"Are you okay?" Anne called loudly.

"I stepped on a nail. It's bleeding pretty bad."

"Come on, let's go," Anne said. "We can doctor it at your house."

Anne was right. What choice did she have? It was over. She was no fortune telling expert. She didn't even have enough foresight to look out for rusty nails. And now she had to figure out a way to explain all this to her mom. What a lousy daughter she was. And a lousy friend—abandoning the quest for Gena's missing retainer, and leading Anne out here to possible danger. Some expert.

She couldn't stay out here and bleed to death, so she slipped off her left sneaker and used the clean sock for a bandage. She placed the bloody sock over it to hold it in place. The left sneaker went on easily over her bare foot, but her right foot was now too bulky and painful to fit into her other shoe. She just put her toes inside the front and lightly crushed the back of the sneaker with her heel, wearing it like a slipper.

Juniper carefully climbed off the boards and limped a few steps in Anne's direction. She could feel the wet sock mushing against her stinging foot, and wondered how she would be able to ride her bike.

"I'm coming," Juniper yelled, knowing this would give Anne some relief.

She hobbled a few steps toward the gate—a noise. Something moved under the boards! She quickly turned back.

"What are you doing?" Anne shouted.

"Anne, go get help!"

Juniper stepped right out of her sneaker and ignored the pain. She rushed to the lumber and started moving the lighter boards out of the way. A buzzing sounded in her head and the tingling returned. She was close, so close. She couldn't stop if she wanted to.

"What are you doing?" Anne asked again.

"Anne, go get help!"

Juniper looked back. Anne hadn't moved. She just stood in one spot, flapping her hands like a baby bird.

The other boards were heavy. She tugged and yanked at them the best she could. She pulled off one after another, scratching and scraping her hands. An image of a tarot card popped into her mind. Strength. She quickly dismissed it. There was no time to think about fortune telling now.

A few boards at the top of the pile came spilling down at Juniper. She threw her arms up to shield herself. Once they stopped, she continued pulling lumber.

One board was particularly hard to move. It felt like concrete.

"What's happening?" Anne called.

Juniper couldn't believe Anne was still there. Why hadn't she gone for help?

A loud creak accompanied the slow movement of the heavy board. Juniper sucked in as much air as she could, but her lungs couldn't hold it in. She heaved the board back and forth to loosen it, huffing with every jerk. Her foot throbbed, but she had to put weight on it for leverage. She managed to pull one end of the board about six inches away from the others. When she did, a small filthy hand slipped through the crack and touched Juniper's fingers. Juniper gasped and fell back. She wanted to laugh, cry, and scream all at once.

"ANNE! GO-GET-HELP!"

CHAPTER 12

To the Rescue

When Juniper looked back, Anne was gone. She held the tiny limp hand in her own and stroked it. "Hang in there, Laurie. Help is on the way." She hoped that was true. Surely Anne would be quick.

An odd feeling touched her—a feeling of connection, and that her own life force was being drawn through her hands and into this squished little girl. It gave her new hope.

She reached for the heavy board again. If she could just move that one, she might give Laurie a little more room. She pulled as hard as she could. The board moved some, but not much. Juniper heard howling again, closer this time. Strange shadows circled her. Small glassy eyes, reflected in the moonlight, peered through the thick weeds. *How many animals are attracted to blood?* she wondered, looking down at the pool around her foot. *Was it the blood, or the creature dying under the boards that attracted them?*

"Hang in there, Laurie," she said again, her voice cracking.

Juniper pulled harder on the board. She scooted it out another six inches, and tried to peek in, but she had left the flashlight in her backpack on the bike. All she could see was Laurie's hand and wrist.

It was then that two large, burly, tattooed arms reached across Juniper and pulled the board. Startled, she jumped back out of the way. Old Man Williams eased the board out with the strength of three men. Juniper helped him pull other boards off. He reached in and gathered the small, crushed body of Laurie Simmons into his arms, then placed her softly on the ground.

Her eyes were closed, her face twisted in pain. Her ragged breaths indicated she was still alive. The sound of distant sirens grew closer. Feeling dizzy, Juniper plopped down on the ground herself and hugged her knees.

Old Man Williams opened the barbed wire gate to let the ambulance and police cars in. Paramedics rushed about with radios and special equipment. Juniper watched as they placed Laurie on a stretcher.

"Her leg is broken," one man reported. They put an oxygen mask on Laurie's face, and an IV needle in her arm. Then they lifted her into the back of the ambulance.

"What about this one?" a paramedic asked, pointing to Juniper.

"We'll call for another ambulance," a policeman answered. "Her mother has already been notified."

Juniper sat up when she heard those words. Right now, she wanted her mom more than anything in the world.

The ambulance drove off, and it wasn't long before the policemen were pushing away a crowd of people. One officer ordered through a blaring bullhorn for them to stay back. A group of reporters arrived and shoved microphones in the police officers' faces.

"Yes, Laurie Simmons has been found," an officer said, "but the details are sketchy at this time."

It was when Juniper's ambulance arrived that the reporters noticed her sitting on the ground. They bombarded her with questions, but she was too weak to answer any of them. Two paramedics put her on a stretcher and began attending to her foot.

"Where's my baby? Where is she?"

At last, the voice Juniper wanted to hear. She stretched out her arms. "Mom!" she called into the crowd.

In an instant, her mom pushed through the bystanders and hugged Juniper tight. Juniper never wanted to let go.

As they lifted her into the ambulance, Juniper saw a few familiar faces in the crowd. One of them was Anne Donovan giving her the thumbs up.

★ ★ ★

Juniper propped her bandaged foot on a pillow and lay back on her bed. She was surrounded by flowers, books, magazines, and the remote control.

"Can I get you anything else?" her mom asked, hovering near the bed.

"Mom, I'm not handicapped," Juniper insisted.

"But the doctor did say for you to stay off that foot for a while."

"If I need anything, I'll tell you," Juniper said. "For goodness sakes, I'm not helpless."

Her dad smiled. "No, that you're not." Luckily, he'd carried his cell phone on the fishing trip.

He patted his daughter on the leg, then turned and walked out.

The doorbell rang.

"If that's another reporter, I'll scream," her mom said, walking out of the bedroom.

Juniper moaned. "Send them away! I couldn't answer another question."

"Well, hello." The tone of Mom's voice meant it wasn't a reporter.

Juniper relaxed when Anne walked in carrying a box of candy. And to her surprise, Gena followed right behind.

"Hello, hero." Anne said with pride.

Although the girls had only been separated for hours, it seemed like an eternity to Juniper. "Boy, am I glad to see you."

"Me or the chocolate?" Anne teased, handing over the candy.

"And you!" Juniper said, giving Gena a puzzled look. "What are you doing here? I thought you were grounded."

Gena flashed her pearly whites. They were wrapped up tight inside her retainer.

"Where did you find it?" Juniper asked.

"The first day I started cleaning my closet, I pulled out an old ski parka. I couldn't decide if I wanted to keep it or not, so I threw it on a chair in my room. My retainer was lying on the chair. I picked up the parka a couple of times when I was looking for it, but my retainer was hung up inside the sleeve. My dad agreed to let me keep the parka, and when I went to hang it up last night, voila!"

"Well, I'm glad it wasn't in the gutter on Park Place Drive," Juniper said.

"Me too!" Gena agreed. "That would have left a real nasty taste in my mouth."

The girls laughed.

Anne stepped forward and handed Juniper an envelope. "I was told to give you this."

Juniper's name was written across the front, and judging by all the curlicues, she knew it was from Beth Wilson.

"The Snotty Twins sent you a card!" Gena grimaced and took a few steps backward as if something might jump out of it and bite her.

Juniper tore into the envelope and pulled out a get-well card. The front had a picture of a sad little panda standing on his head. When she opened it up, out fell six pink Band-Aids with red hearts. Written inside were the words *"Hope You're Back on Your Feet Soon."* It was signed by Beth and Nicole.

She held up one of the Band-Aids and rolled her eyes. "I'd bleed to death before I'd wear one of these."

"Come on," Anne said. "Be nice."

"Yeah," Gena agreed. "Look on the bright side. Your sock will cover them up."

Juniper laughed out loud, but quickly covered her mouth when she saw Anne's threatening looks. She glanced at the card and the Band-Aids and grinned. "I guess a crisis like this can bring even the worst of enemies together. I'll have to call them and say thanks."

"So, have you heard anything new about Laurie Simmons?" Anne asked.

"Last I heard, they updated her condition from critical to serious. That's a good sign. She was totally dehydrated, and suffering from heat stroke and shock, not to mention her broken leg."

Gena sat cross-legged on the bed. "Does anyone know exactly what happened? I keep hearing different stories on the news."

"From what I've heard, she ran away to the lumberyard because she thought it was a good place to hide. She was pulling on that stack of lumber when it fell down on her. The doctors think it must have knocked her unconscious for a while because no one heard her yell for help. I guess the truth will come out when she's better. Her parents came by my hospital room before I left this morning to thank me. They were both really nice. Oh yeah—and guess who else came to see me."

Anne and Gena looked clueless. "Who?" Anne asked.

A big grin dimpled Juniper's cheeks. "Mr. Williams."

There was a moment of silence before a light flashed on in Gena's eyes. "Old Man Williams?"

"*Mr.* Williams said I was very brave, even though I'm a little nuts in the head. And you know what? After talking to him up close, I don't think he's any older than my dad. Just a little grubbier."

"So the rumors aren't true," Anne said.

Gena stamped her foot on the floor. "Well, heck, now we'll have to find another old geezer for all those urban legends."

"Or maybe we should just let all those tall tales die out," Juniper suggested.

"By the way, I saw your mom on the news too," Gena said. "Boy, it sounds like she's really on a crusade to get that lumberyard cleaned up."

"And she won't stop until it's done!" Juniper put in.

Just then, Juniper's mom walked in with two pain tablets and a glass of water. "You don't have to take these right away," she said. "But don't let the pain get too unbearable." She handed Juniper the glass and walked out.

"So, Madam Juniper, the all-knowing, all-seeing," Gena said, pointing to the glass of water, "what do you see in our future?"

"That's easy," Juniper answered, holding the glass high. "A really great summer!"

DOTTI ENDERLE

Dotti Enderle has been telling fortunes since before she was born. She is extremely psychic as she always knows when there is chocolate nearby. She lives in Texas with her husband, two daughters, and a lazy cat named Oliver. Find out more about Dotti and her books at:

www.fortunetellersclub.com

Here's a glimpse of what's ahead in Fortune Tellers Club #2, *Playing with Fire*

CHAPTER 3

The Scoop

The buzz in the school cafeteria was typical for a Friday. The kids were yapping a little too loudly, but the teachers were so happy for the end of the week, they ignored it.

Anne sat across from Juniper and Gena. They'd been talking through most of lunch, but Anne barely kept up with what they said. Eric was sitting at the table right behind her.

"So, what about it?" Gena said, stuffing her dirty napkin, sandwich bag, bent straw, empty raisin box, and a candy wrapper into her drained milk carton.

"What about what?" Anne asked.

Juniper sighed. "Are you going with us to the movies tomorrow afternoon or not?"

"Yeah, I'll go," Anne said. "But not early. I need to make out my birthday invitations sometime this weekend."

"That's right," Gena said. "Soon you'll be able to tell us what it's like to be thirteen. Are you inviting a bunch of people?"

"Are you ready for this?" Anne asked, barely able to hold it in. "It took me four hours, but I finally talked my mom into letting me have a boy-girl party."

"No way!" Juniper said.

"Can you believe it? I'm so excited." Anne meant it. She was more than excited. She was ready to turn cartwheels.

Juniper started gathering her empty things too. "I can't go to the movies early, either. I have that audition in the morning."

"Oh yeah," Anne said. "What production is your dance studio doing this year?

"It's a jazzed up version of *The Nutcracker Suite*. It's going to be fun, but I'm a little nervous. I'm trying out for the lead."

Gena nudged her. "You're the best dancer at your studio. Who could possibly beat you out?"

Juniper slumped. "Nicole Hoffman."

"Uh-oh, she's a good dancer," Anne said. She turned her gaze to the end of the table where Nicole sat with Beth and a couple of other girls. The two were whispering, and snickering, and covering their mouths.

"She's not as good as you," Gena said. "As a matter of fact, I predict that she'll fall on her rear so many times they'll have to change the name of the production to *The Buttcracker Suite*."

Anne and Juniper roared with laughter. Anne even snorted, then covered her mouth. Eric was right behind her. Did he hear that? How embarrassing. She tried to turn her head slightly to see what he was up to, but didn't want to be obvious.

"Go ahead," Gena said. "Turn around and look at him. You've been dying to all during lunch."

"What's he doing?" Anne whispered.

"He's looking at you," Gena said.

"No, seriously."

"Seriously," Juniper said. "He's looking at you."

Anne sat up straight. She knew Juniper wouldn't tease. She wished she were sitting on the other side so she could see. "Why do you think he's looking at me?"

"Maybe he needs to borrow some more money," Gena said.

"Come on, he paid me back."

Gena leaned in. "By the way, you do know that he lives in the same apartment complex as me?"

"Why didn't you tell me before?" Anne asked, throwing her wadded up napkin at Gena.

"Because I didn't know until yesterday."

"And you're just now telling me!"

"Hey, I didn't think it was an emergency." Gena said. "But he has a great apartment number—1313."

Juniper's eyes grew big. "Spooky."

"It gets spookier," Gena whispered.

Anne and Juniper leaned in even more. Anne hoped that whatever Gena was going to say would be another one of her jokes. She couldn't bear to think there was something wrong with Eric.

"You know why he transferred here and is living in an apartment?"

Anne shook her head.

"His house in Brookhaven burned down. To the ground. Incinerated. Ashes-to-ashes."

"That's not spooky, that's sad," Juniper said.

"Yes, but there's more." Gena grinned like she knew every secret in the world.

"I heard he set the fire."